THE STORIES OF
PINOCCHIO
AND OTHER TALES

THE STORIES OF
PINOCCHIO
AND OTHER TALES

NEW YORK

CONTENTS

Cover illustration by Francis Phillipps
Cover design by Kasa and Steel

Copyright © Marshall Cavendish 1982, 1983, 1984
This edition © 1987 by Marshall Cavendish Limited

First published in USA 1987 by Exeter Books
Distributed by Bookthrift
Exeter is a trademark of Bookthrift Marketing, Inc.
Bookthrift is a registered trademark of Bookthrift Marketing, Inc.
New York, New York

ALL RIGHTS RESERVED

ISBN 0-671-08498-4

Printed and bound in Vicenza, Italy by L.E.G.O.

In Italy, about a hundred years ago, there lived a wood-carver named Geppetto. He was a very poor man, and he lived on his own. Although Geppetto had friendly neighbours, he was lonely at heart and he wished he had a son.

One day he had an idea. He decided to make himself a wooden puppet — a wonderful puppet that would know how to dance and fight and leap like an acrobat. With this puppet, Geppetto could travel the world. People everywhere would pay a lot to see them perform their tricks. But, more important, it would be like a son to him and keep him company.

Straight away, Geppetto chose a log from his wood pile, took his sharpest axe and set to work. But just as he aimed his first blow, he heard a very small voice. "Don't hit me too hard, please!"

You can imagine how surprised the old man was. He looked at the log, he looked all round the room — he even opened the door and looked outside. But he could see no-one. So he started again, just a little more carefully.

All went well as Geppetto stripped off the bark. But when he took his plane to smooth and polish the wood, he heard the same voice breaking out in giggles, "Stop it. Oh, stop it! You're tickling me!" And Geppetto dropped his plane as if he had been struck by a bolt of lightning.

The wood-carver sank into his rickety chair and stared blankly at the

So he chiselled away merrily. Geppetto whistled as he worked, and thought up a name for his puppet. "I'll call him Pinocchio," he decided. "It's a good name — it will bring him luck."

First Geppetto made the head, then he shaped the the forehead, then the eyes, and then the nose. It was there that things started going strangely wrong. The nose began to grow! And it grew and grew and

piece of wood. He stared and he stared, until it seemed he had been gazing for hours. He scratched his head and he rubbed his chin. He crossed his legs and drummed his fingers on the table. He puffed at his pipe. Then he knocked out the ash and grabbed the log again.

"Well, this couldn't be better," he said to himself at last. "Here I am, making a puppet, and before I have even carved his head, he's talking! By the time I've finished him, he'll be able to walk and run and dance and sing!"

6

grew. Poor Geppetto tired himself out chopping the nose down to size.

As for the mouth, it started laughing at Geppetto before it was even finished, and then stuck out a tongue at him as far as it would go!

Geppetto was alarmed, but he pretended not to notice. He pressed on with his work, and fashioned the puppet's body and arms. Then no sooner had he cut out the hands than they pulled his moustache.

"Stop him! Stop him! shouted Geppetto, as he rushed after Pinocchio. But the people were so amazed to see a wooden puppet running down the street that they could hardly move for laughing. The local policeman had more sense. He stepped out into the street and when the puppet tried to dash between his legs he picked him up by his nose.

Poor Geppetto felt more miserable than he had ever felt in his life. What sort of a son was he making for himself? "You young scamp! You're not even finished and already you're being rude to your father! That is bad, very bad." And he wiped a tear from his eye.

There was worse to come. As soon as Geppetto finished off the puppet's legs and feet, Pinocchio gave him a kick on the chin, sprang down to the floor and ran out of the door and away along the street.

up in the police station for the night. Well, Pinocchio was free as a bird, and he scampered off, dancing and leaping and clicking his heels together. He played for hours in the streets and went back home when the sun was setting. He pushed the door open, and threw himself down in Geppetto's old chair by the fireside. Outside, darkness was falling, and it was turning windy and cold, but Pinocchio sat grinning with pleasure. He was warm and cosy — and on the very first day of his life he was his own master.

Geppetto was grumbling furiously when he reached them. He seized Pinocchio by the neck and hauled him off down the road. "You just wait till we get home. I'll soon show you what happens to naughty boys."

Pinocchio wriggled free and threw himself to the ground, sobbing pathetically. Before Geppetto knew what was happening, all the people were calling to the policeman. "Protect the poor puppet, or Geppetto will kill him!" And they set up such a storm of protest that Geppetto was arrested and locked

But Pinocchio was not alone in the room. As he lay back in the chair and closed his eyes, he heard a rapid clicking noise, like the teeth of a comb being scraped on a table's edge, "Cri-cri-cri-cri-cri."

"Who's there?" said Pinocchio.

"It is I." Pinocchio turned round and saw a big insect crawling slowly along the wall. "I am the Talking Cricket, and I have lived in this room for a hundred years and more."

"So what! It's my room now, so just buzz off and leave me alone."

"I will not go until I have told you a great truth," replied the cricket. "Boys who rebel against their parents never come to any good in the world, and sooner or later they will be bitterly sorry for what they have done."

This was the last thing Pinocchio wanted to hear. "Hold your tongue, you silly croaker. Go away."

But the cricket took no notice. "Poor Pinocchio, I pity you. You really *do* have a wooden head, and what is more you will come to a bad end."

At these words, Pinocchio lost his temper. He snatched Geppetto's mallet from the work-bench and hurled it at the cricket. Maybe he didn't mean to hurt him, but the mallet hit the little creature right on the head and he scarcely had time to cry out before he fell limply to the ground. "That's shut you up," said Pinocchio, and he tried to go to sleep.

It was the start of a miserable night for the wicked puppet. No sooner had Pinocchio closed his eyes than he began

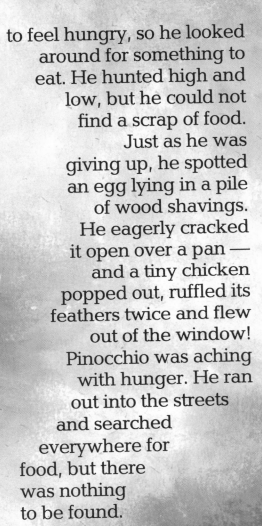

to feel hungry, so he looked around for something to eat. He hunted high and low, but he could not find a scrap of food. Just as he was giving up, he spotted an egg lying in a pile of wood shavings. He eagerly cracked it open over a pan — and a tiny chicken popped out, ruffled its feathers twice and flew out of the window! Pinocchio was aching with hunger. He ran out into the streets and searched everywhere for food, but there was nothing to be found.

floor, he felt very sorry for him, and gave his son the three pears he had bought for his own breakfast. Then he placed him gently on the work-bench, and lovingly carved him a new pair of feet. After they were finished, the old wood-carver cut out a special set of clothes for Pinocchio: a pair of short trousers, a colourful shirt of flowered paper, and a cap made from a crust of bread.

In desperation, he rang on a neighbour's doorbell to beg for a meal. But a crotchety old man, angry at being disturbed in the middle of the night, poured a great basin of water all over him.

Pinocchio slunk home like a drowned rat, so cold and exhausted that he flopped down in the chair with his feet in the hearth. For the rest of the night he slept and snored — and all the time his wooden feet were in the fire. Little by little they burned away to cinders. By the morning he could not even stand up.

Geppetto came back from the gaol fuming with anger. But when he saw poor Pinocchio, crawling around on the

Pinocchio was so relieved to be able to walk again, and so excited with his new clothes, that he leapt up from the work-bench, threw his arms around Geppetto's neck, and kissed him again and again. "Oh please help me, Daddy," he sobbed, and he poured out the story of the cricket's warning. "Don't let me come to a bad end — I do *want* to be good."

They hugged each other for a long time. Finally Geppetto spoke through his tears. "If you *really* want to be a good boy, Pinocchio, you must go to school and work hard."

"Oh I will," cried Pinocchio. "I will! I promise I will."

The Puppet Theatre

Pinocchio had promised Geppetto he would be a good puppet and go to school. But first he needed a spelling book, and the wood-carver was so poor that he had no money to by one. Geppetto pulled out his pockets one by one. Then looked in the rusty old tin on his work-bench. But there was not a penny anywhere. With a deep sigh, he put on his coat and went to the door. "Wait for me here, Pinocchio," he said, and disappeared round the corner.

A few minutes later he was back with a spelling book — but without his coat. He had sold it in exchange of the book.

Pinocchio kissed his father again, and thanked him. Then he hurried off to school.

As Pinocchio marched along, all sorts of grand ideas ran through his head.

"Today I shall learn to read," he said to himself, "then tomorrow I'll learn writing, and the next day arithmetic. Then I'll earn lots of money and buy my dear father a beautiful new coat." There was no end to his good intentions — until he heard the sound of drums and trumpets in the distance.

The music was coming from a brightly painted building, and a large sign announced *Puppet Theatre*. At the entrance stood a man beating a drum to announce the start of a performance, and crowds of people were pushing their way into the hall.

Pinocchio could not wait to join them. "How much does it cost to go in?" he asked. "Only two pence to a young lad like you," replied the man outside.

Within seconds Pinocchio had sold the schoolbook to a street trader , bought a ticket and dashed into the theatre.

Imagine his delight when he saw the actors! There were Harlequin and Punch, quarrelling as usual and whacking each other with big sticks. The audience was roaring with laughter. Then Punch caught sight of Pinocchio and there was almost a riot. "It's our little wooden brother," he shouted. "Come up here and join us!" And all the other puppets rushed on to the stage to greet Pinocchio.

What a sight it was! They hugged him and kissed him, gave him friendly pats and pinches, and ended up carrying him in triumph across the stage.

But the audience was not amused. They set up a tremendous racket. *"We want the play! We want the play!"*

Fire-Eater looked hard at Pinocchio, and he suddenly sneezed. It was a sure sign that his pity had been aroused. "All right, free him. And throw Harlequin on the fire instead. I must have my meat well roasted!"

Just think of poor Harlequin! He had saved Pinocchio, only to die himself! His knees buckled under him, and his head flopped forward. Two of the soldier puppets seized his arms and dragged him towards the flames.

At this awful sight! Pinocchio threw himself down before the puppet-master. "Have pity, Sir Fire-Eater! Pardon brave Harlequin. He has done you no wrong!"

"Impossible! The fire is already low and I must have my meat well roasted."

"In that case," said Pinocchio, "I know my duty. It's not right that

Suddenly, silence fell. The puppet-master, a ferocious looking giant called Fire-Eater with a long beard as black as ink, had burst on to the stage. His eyes were like burning coals, and in his hand was a hideous whip made of snakes and foxes' tails.

"Why do you dare to come into my theatre?" he bellowed. And he siezed Pinocchio and threw him into a log basket in the kitchen. The play started again, and when it finished Fire-Eater called to Punch, "bring that puppet here and throw it on the fire! I must have a good blaze to get my meat well roasted for supper!"

Pinocchio was brought in, struggling for his life and calling for help. Then his brother Harlequin went down on one knee. "O Fire-Eater," he cried, "spare our little brother. He's much too young to die."

Harlequin should die for me. Puppets, bind me and throw *me* into the flames!"

At these words, all the puppets burst into tears. How noble Pinocchio was! And how dreadful that he should come to a bad end! Then, suddenly, the room echoed to a deafening noise. Fire-Eater had sneezed again, not once but three times! And when he finally stopped he lifted Pinocchio into his arms.

"You're a good boy! Harlequin shall be freed, and tonight, just this once, I will have to eat my mutton half cooked."

Sitting Pinocchio on his knee, he asked him where he had

come from, and who his father was. And when he heard that Geppetto was just a poor wood-carver, he began sneezing all over again. "Here, take these five gold pieces and give them to your father. And tell him to keep a better eye on you in the future! Now get home before I change my mind."

Pinocchio left the hall with the cheers of the puppets ringing in his ears. He was as happy as could be — now he could buy another schoolbook *and* give Geppetto a brand new coat. He whistled cheerfully as he marched back along the road, and at every step he tossed a coin high into the air, catching it as it fell.

He could hardly wait to see Geppetto's face!

Little did he know what fate had in store for him, or how long a journey he had begun. For he had not gone far when he met two travellers — a Fox, who was lame in one foot, and a Cat, who was blind in both eyes. These unfortunate creatures were helping each other along, the Fox leaning on the Cat's shoulder and showing him the way.

"Good day," said the Fox, politely.

"Good day, Mr Fox," replied Pinocchio, spinning a coin casually in the air.

The gold coin flashed in the sunlight. The Fox's lame paw twitched a little, and the Cat's blind eyes opened wide like two green lamps — but only for a fraction of a second.

"I say!" said the Fox as they all walked along together. "What a lot of money you have. And what will you spend it on, if I may ask?"

Naturally Pinocchio was very interested, especially when the Cat explained that doubling your money was child's play. If you knew how, you could easily turn five gold coins into 500, or even 5,000!

"All you have to do," the Cat continued, "is to bury your money in the Field of Miracles. You water it, salt it, leave it for two hours, and then what do you find? Your money has grown into a magnificent tree, laden with hundreds of bright new coins."

Instantly, Pinocchio forgot all about his father, the new coat and the schoolbook. All he could think of was the wonderful Field of Miracles. He just *had* to see it. And at the very next turning the Fox and the Cat led him away down a narrow winding lane and out into the country.

"First I shall buy a new coat for my father, and then I shall buy a spelling book. I'm going to school, to learn to be good."

"Oh dear," said the Fox. "Look at me. Through my long years of study I have lost the use of my paw."

"And look at me," said the Cat. "Through my long years of study I have gone blind!"

At that very moment, a blackbird perched in the hedge called out a warning. "Pinocchio, don't listen to those bad men . . ." But before he could finish, the Cat sprang on the bird and gulped him down in a single mouthful, feathers and all.

"Nothing but trouble, blackbirds," sneered the Cat.

They were all halfway to Pinocchio's house when the Fox suddenly stopped. "How would you like to double your money?" he asked.

The Field of Miracles

With his two shady companions, the Fox and the Cat, Pinocchio was still trudging along when the sun went down.

"Look!" said the Fox suddenly. "There's the Red Crab Inn. We can have a bite to eat, then press on at midnight to arrive at the Field of Miracles by dawn tomorrow!"

But when they sat down at the table, none of them, it seemed, had any appetite. The Cat could only squeeze down thirty-five helpings of fish and four helpings of tripe, while the Fox struggled gamely with a few dozen partridges, six rabbits and a hare. Pinocchio ate nothing at all — could think only of the great day to come.

After their snack, the Fox ordered rooms for the three of them, and they all went off to sleep, leaving firm instructions to be woken at midnight. But when the inn-keeper shook Pinocchio awake, he had strange news.

"The Fox and the Cat have been called away early. They will meet you at the Field of Miracles at sunrise, if you make your own way there. Oh, and would you mind paying the bill for all three of you . . .?"

Pinocchio handed over one of his five precious gold coins and hurried on his way.

Dark clouds covered the stars, so he whistled to help keep up his spirits. Everything seemed very eerie. Then, as the road led through a dense wood, Pinocchio heard a rusle of leaves behind him! There in the gloom were two hooded figures — and they were chasing him!

The robbers were catching up fast, so Pinocchio popped the four gold coins into his mouth and scrambled up a tree. Surely he would be safe

there! But looking down, he saw the robbers set fire to the tree, and in no time at all flames were darting up towards him.

Pinocchio made a huge leap down on to the ground and raced away again. He sprang across a large ditch, and turned to see the robbers fall in! But they were out again in a trice, and following as fast as ever. Then, as Pinocchio felt he could run no further, he saw a little cottage and staggered towards it. Just before he reached the door, powerful hands seized him by the throat and a hollow voice demanded, "Your money — or your life!"

Pinocchio shook his head. "Come on now, no nonsense! Where's that money? Tell us or we'll kill you!"

"No, no!" cried poor Pinocchio — and the coins clinked in his mouth.

"So, you cheat! The money is under your tongue. Well, we know how to shake it out of there!" And with a horrible noise, like a Fox snarling, the taller of the two robbers pulled a noose from under his cloak and slipped it over Pinocchio's head. Seconds later, the poor puppet was dangling from the nearest tree.

The two robbers slunk away. "We'll be back tomorrow, when you'll be dead, with your mouth hanging open."

As Pinocchio's flimsy body swung in the night wind, he thought of all the warnings he had been given, until his breath failed him and he hung stiff and silent.

Now, the owner of the cottage was a beautiful Fairy, who had lived in the wood for more than a thousand years. And she had seen everything from her window. As soon as the robbers were out of sight the Fairy sent her very best carriage, driven by a poodle and drawn by a hundred pairs of white mice, to bring the limp body of Pinocchio to the cottage.

Soon, at his bedside, stood three worried doctors — and owl, a crow and a cricket — discussing their patient. And what should Pinocchio hear first as he woke, but the voice of the cricket. "I've seen that puppet before. He's a good-for-nothing rogue, a disobedient son who will make his poor father die of a broken heart."

Pinocchio burst into tears, But the sound of his sobs made the doctors happy, for their patient was obviously alive. "When a *dead* person cries, it is a sign that he is getting much better," droned the owl. "I think we may leave now, gentlemen." And out of the door they went.

Then the Fairy felt Pinocchio's forehead. He still had a high temperature and was very ill, so she made him some medicine. But because it was bitter, the puppet refused to take it. And when the Fairy gave him sugar to sweeten the taste, he crunched down the sugar and refused the medicine!

At that the door swung open and four black rabbits entered the room, carrying a coffin for Pinocchio.

"We have come to take you away," said the head rabbit.

"To take me?" squealed Pinocchio. "But I'm not dead! Fairy, oh Fairy, give me the medicine, please!" And Pinocchio downed the bitter liquid in one swallow.

"What a waste of out time," grumbled the rabbits. "That's another journey made for nothing." And they all trooped out of the room muttering.

A few minutes later, Pinocchio was well again. This is quite normal, you know. Wooden puppets are not often ill for long!

He told the Fairy the whole story and boasted about how clever he had been to hide the gold under his tongue.

"But where's the gold now?" asked the Fairy.

"Um, I've lost it!" said Pinocchio — and at once his nose began to grow!

"And where exactly did you lose it?"

"Um, in the wood." And his nose grew even more. "No, I remember. I didn't lose it. I swallowed it." And with that enormous fib his nose grew so long

that he could not turn around. If he turned left, his nose struck the bed. And if he turned right it hit the window-pane!

"You're lying, Pinocchio," smiled the Fairy. And she explained to him that every time he told a lie his nose would grow. Poor Pinocchio was in misery, and the Fairy had to stifle her laughter. So she called a flock of woodpeckers to trim his enormous nose back to its usual size.

"How kind you are, Fairy," he said humbly. "I love you so much."

"I love you to, Pinocchio, and I will always look after you. But now you must forget all about the Field of Miracles and go home to your father, Geppetto. He is worried to death about you."

half a day, they came to a town called Trap o' Fools, where the streets were crowded with hundreds of poor beggars. And a mile further on they reached an empty field — a field that looked exactly like every other field they had passed.

"Here we are at last," puffed the Fox "Now kneel down and dig a little hole. That's it, now put the coins in. Sprinkle this pinch of salt over them, and fill the hole again."

"Is that all I have to do?"

"Well, just pour on a little water. Good, that's perfect. We'll all go away now, but if you come back in two hours' time you'll find a thick bush poking through the ground, with its branches weighed down with gold!"

Pinocchio could not thank his friends enough. He wanted them to stay, and take at least a thousand of the new coins as a reward for their help. But the Cat would not hear of it. "We need no reward. It's quite enough for us to see you so wealthy and contended." So saying, they all shook hands and parted on the very best of terms.

Pinocchio walked back to Trap o'

So Pinocchio kissed the Fairy goodbye and hurried off through the wood. But just as he was passing the tree where the robbers had strung him up, who should he meet but the Fox and Cat.

"Why, here is our dear Pinocchio," cried the Fox, hugging him tight. "What are you doing here?"

"Yes, what are you doing here?" asked the Cat.

Pinocchio told his story once again, while the two crafty animals pretended to be amazed. How sad they were to hear his tale! And how helpful they would be!

You can guess what happened. In no time at all Pinocchio had forgotten Geppetto and set off for the Field of Miracles with the Fox and the Cat.

After a long march, which took them

Fools and counted the minutes on the church clock. When the two hours were nearly up he hurried off to collect his gold. His head was full of plans about how he would spend the money and help Geppetto. But when he entered the field again, he could see nothing. Absolutely nothing.

coins and fled like the wind!"

With the shrieks of the parrot ringing in his ears, Pinocchio hurried back to Trap o' Fools and went straight to the Law Court to demand justice. He was called before the chief judge, a wise old gorilla, and accused the Cat and the Fox of fraud and robbery. When the judge had heard

With an awful sinking feeling in his stomach, Pinocchio ran to the place where he had buried the coins. The hole had been dug open again, and was completely empty! As Pinocchio fell to his knees in despair he heard a low cackle of laughter from the tree behind him. Looking round he saw a large parrot, preening its feathers.

"Ah, what a fool you are, I nearly died laughing when I saw you plant that gold. That crafty old Fox and Cat came back while you were away, dug up the

the evidence, he rapped his mallet on the table and passed judgement.

"You are a fool, Pinocchio, and fools must be trapped. Since you have lost *four* gold coins, you will go straight to jail and stay there *four* months." And with a hollow clang, the prison doors slammed shut on poor Pinocchio, the puppet who just could not be good.

After four long months in prison, Pinocchio was finally set free. And when the iron doors swung open his only thought was to hurry away from the horrible Trap o' Fools. First he would visit the Fairy, and then he would go home to his father, Geppetto.

The road was muddy from days of rain but Pinocchio skipped along merrily until, turning a corner, he found his way completely blocked. An enormous snake with glaring red eyes, and smoke billowing from its tail lay right across the path!

Pinocchio was too scared to try and pass the snake, so he waited at a safe distance for it to move. But the snake just stayed where it was, staring at him with its fiery eyes. At last, Pinocchio summoned up all his courage, walked right up to the snake, and asked very politely if it would let him pass. To his amazement, the snake immediately lay down and closed its eyes — even its tail stopped smoking. "He must be dead," thought Pinocchio, and he tried to jump over the body. But just as he took off, the snake reared up angrily and Pinocchio was thrown backwards and landed head down in the mud!

The snake had only been playing, and now it burst into a great fit of giggles at the sight of the puppet's wriggling, upside-down body. But it laughed so much at its own joke that it suddenly split its sides . . . and collapsed!

This time the snake really *was* dead, so Pinocchio picked himself up, clambered over it, and ran on down the path. After all the excitement he felt very hungry, so when he saw some juicy grapes growing in a field, he climbed over the fence to pick a bunch. It was a big mistake, for just as he was stretching out his hand there was a loud crack — as the jaws of a hideous iron trap snapped fast around his legs.

Poor Pinocchio screamed and yelled for hours, but no-one came. Then, through the gloom, a farmer appeared.

"Well, well, what have we got here? Ha! So it's you that's been catching my chickens! And I thought it was weasels!"

"It wasn't me, really it wasn't! I only wanted some grapes!"

"Anyone who steals grapes is quite capable of stealing chickens. You're coming with me to the farmyard. My guard-dog died this morning, so you can take his place!"

And, to Pinocchio's horror, the farmer buckled a heavy dog collar around his neck and chained him to a kennel!

"If you see any of those thieving weasels you bark at once! Understand?" Then the farmer went off to bed, leaving the puppet with a bowl of water and an old bone.

Pinocchio lay down on the straw. Oh, how miserable he was! Finally he cried himself to sleep, but soon he was woken by strange noises. There, right inside the farmyard, were four large weasels. One of them tip-toed over to the kennel.

"Evening, Melampo."

"I'm not Melampo. He's dead. I'm a puppet, and I'm here as a punishment."

"Never mind, never mind. We'll give you the same deal as we had with Melampo. If you keep quiet, and let us take eight chickens each week, there'll be one plump chicken for you. All right?"

"Well, I'm . . ." and before Pinocchio could say more, the weasels had opened the door to the chicken-house nearby and slipped inside.

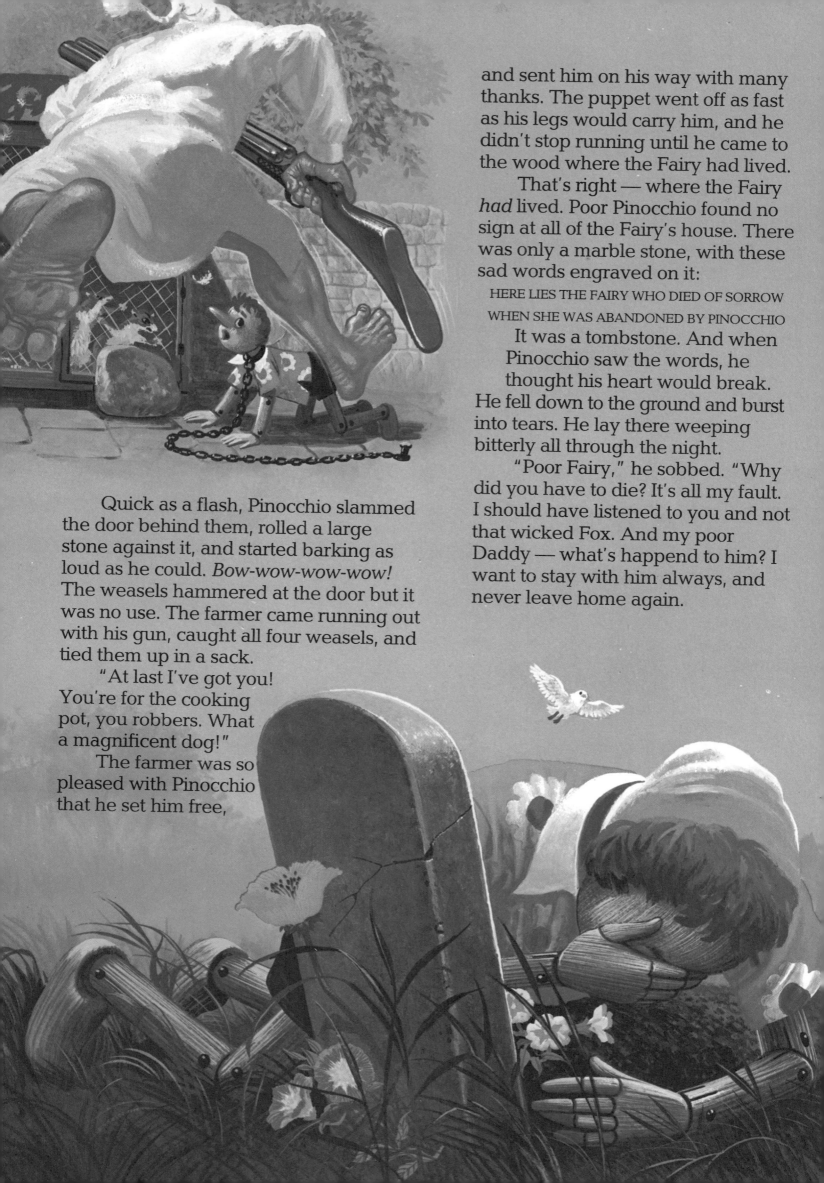

and sent him on his way with many thanks. The puppet went off as fast as his legs would carry him, and he didn't stop running until he came to the wood where the Fairy had lived.

That's right — where the Fairy *had* lived. Poor Pinocchio found no sign at all of the Fairy's house. There was only a marble stone, with these sad words engraved on it:

HERE LIES THE FAIRY WHO DIED OF SORROW
WHEN SHE WAS ABANDONED BY PINOCCHIO

It was a tombstone. And when Pinocchio saw the words, he thought his heart would break. He fell down to the ground and burst into tears. He lay there weeping bitterly all through the night.

"Poor Fairy," he sobbed. "Why did you have to die? It's all my fault. I should have listened to you and not that wicked Fox. And my poor Daddy — what's happend to him? I want to stay with him always, and never leave home again.

Quick as a flash, Pinocchio slammed the door behind them, rolled a large stone against it, and started barking as loud as he could. *Bow-wow-wow-wow!* The weasels hammered at the door but it was no use. The farmer came running out with his gun, caught all four weasels, and tied them up in a sack.

"At last I've got you! You're for the cooking pot, you robbers. What a magnificent dog!"

The farmer was so pleased with Pinocchio that he set him free,

"Oh Fairy, please come back to life. Don't leave me here alone."

And Pinocchio wished that he could die himself.

Then, in the green light of dawn, a huge dove flew overhead. Hovering above the tombstone, it called down to the puppet, "Is that you, Pinocchio? I have been looking for you everywhere." And when Pinocchio nodded sadly, the great bird landed behind him, breathless with news.

"You must come quickly! Your father Geppetto is about to sail away. You have been lost so long he thought you must have gone to another land. He has built himself a boat, to cross the ocean and search for you."

Pinocchio sprang on to the dove's back and away they flew, soaring high above the clouds. He was so scared of falling that he hung on tightly with both hands. There was a long, long way to go, so they flew all day, and they flew all night. And early the next morning the dove left Pinocchio on a stony beach.

A crowd of people were there, shouting and waving out to sea. "What's happened?" cried Pinocchio. "Tell me, please." An old woman explained. "A father has set out in a tiny boat to find his lost son. But now the storm has blown up and he is sure to drown!"

Pinocchio scrambled up a high rock and stared out to sea. Sure enough, there in the distance, was Geppetto, waving helplessly back to shore. "Daddy, I'm coming!" shouted Pinocchio. "I'll save you!" But at that very moment a huge wave crashed down on the boat, and it was seen no more.

became calm. He laid his clothes out to dry in the sun, and sat gazing across the water for Geppetto's little boat. Wherever he looked he could see nothing. But then a large fish came swimming round the bay, close to the shore.

"Excuse me, Mr Fish," called Pinocchio.

"Yes, young man," replied the fish, who was in fact a Dolphin, and very friendly.

"Have you see a little boat with my Daddy in it?"

"Oh dear," said the Dolphin, "was that your father? During the storm he and his boat were swallowed by a shark. You poor boy — you won't see him again, I'm afraid!" And he swam sadly away.

Pinocchio dived into the foaming waters and swam through the storm. He floated easily because he was made of wood, but the wind soon blew him off course. The rain lashed the sea in torrents, thunder crashed and lightning split the sky. Hour after hour the puppet was hurled about like a bundle of sticks — and then one enormous wave lifted him clear out of the water and dumped him down on a sandy shore.

Pinocchio lay exhausted on the beach as, little by little, the sky cleared and the sea

Poor Pinocchio. First he loses the Fairy, and now his father, Geppetto. He put his clothes on, and with his heart as heavy as lead followed the road away from the beach. After an hour he came to a place called Busy Bee Village, where the streets were full of people all working at their trades. Wherever he looked there was not a single person idle.

"This won't suit me," thought Pinocchio. "I hate working."

By now he was very thirsty, so he asked a young woman, who was carrying two pails of water, if he could have a drink.

"Of course you can. Here, drink up." And Pinocchio guzzled as if he had never drunk water before.

"And I'll give you some bread and stew if you'll help me with these pails."

"But I hate working. I'm not a donkey, you know!"

"*And* some syrup pudding!"

Pinocchio was so ravenous he could not resist. "All right then. I'll carry this smaller one to your house."

They struggled up the road with the heavy pails, and as soon as they were inside her house the woman gave Pinocchio his bread and stew and syrup pudding. He gobbled them down as if he had never eaten before.

When he had finished he looked up at the young woman — and there before him was the very face, with the same hair and the same eyes, that he had thought never to see again.

"O Fairy, it's *you*! You're *alive*! I thought I'd lost you for ever, like Daddy. I've been so unhappy — *please* don't make me cry again."

And he threw himself down on the floor and hugged her knees.

The Fairy smiled and stroked his head, then she picked him up and kissed him.

"I'm glad to see you too, Pinocchio. Will you stay with me now, like a good boy?" "Yes, I promise!"

Pinocchio had settled down happily at the Fairy's house on Busy Bee Island. But something was bothering him. "I'm fed up with being a puppet," he suddenly said one day. "I want to become a *real* boy, and grow up to be a man!"

"Oh, that won't be so easy," replied the Fairy. "Puppets never grow. But if you are very good perhaps we can make an exception — if you deserve it. No more lies, mind, and no more lazing about round here! You'll have to go to school, and work hard!"

"You mean I *can* become a *real* boy?" shouted Pinocchio, dancing with glee.

"If you work hard for a whole year and stop all your naughty habits, I promise that you will become a real boy. So off you go to school, tomorrow!"

You can imagine what it was like when he first arrived.

The other boys thought it was hilarious to have a puppet in their class, and they played all kinds of nasty tricks on him. But when they pulled Pinocchio's long nose, he set about them with his wooden feet and wooden fists until they learned to show some respect.

Within a few weeks he was friends with almost everyone. But there was one thing the others still held against him — he was already top of the class.

30

So one fine day, some of them stopped Pinocchio on his way to school and told him that a huge whale had been seen near the coast. "We're going to sneak off school and see for ourselves. Why don't you come along too?"

Pinocchio wanted to wait until after school, but the boys all laughed at him. "The whale won't wait all day for you!"

So, once again, poor Pinocchio was led astray. But it was not long before he realised he had been completely fooled. There was no whale to be seen, and the sea was as smooth as a mirror.

"He must have gone off for his breakfast!" jeered one of the boys. "Or perhaps he's having a nap! laughed another.

Pinocchio was furious. And the more the boys laughed at him, the angrier he got. Before you knew it, a great fight had broken out and schoolbooks and satchels were being thrown in all directions.

In all the confusion, one of the boys was struck on the forehead by a flying book and sank to the ground, as white as a sheet. At this dreadful sight, the other boys ran off as fast as they could, leaving Pinocchio alone with their fallen friend.

The puppet was still there, bathing the boy's head with a handkerchief soaked in sea-water, when two policemen appeared behind him with a dog. "You'd better come along with us. This boy is badly hurt. You're under arrest." And summoning an old man from a nearby cottage to care for the injured boy, they dragged Pinocchio back along the road towards town.

The little puppet
was absolutely terrified.
His legs trembled and his
tongue stuck to the roof of his
mouth so that he could not speak —
even to tell them *he* had not thrown
the book. But just as he thought
he would die of fright, a gust of
wind blew his cap back towards the
beach. The policemen let him run after it,
and Pinocchio seized his chance to escape!

    This only made matters worse. The
policemen unleashed their prize bulldog
— a huge savage beast called Alidoro.
Soon Pinocchio could hear it panting close
behind him. Then he could feel the dog's
hot breath on the back of his legs. Now he
was almost at the cliff edge . . . and with a
last desperate leap, he flung himself into
the waves and swam out.

        Alidoro tried hard to stop,
            digging his paws into
            the ground, but his
            speed carried him

deep into the water. The poor dog could
not swim! He struggled to keep afloat, but
it was no good. As he came to the surface
for the third time, his eyes were rolling
with terror and he barked piteously.
"Help me, Pinocchio! Save me from
drowning!"

    When he heard this feeble cry,
Pinocchio's heart melted. He swam
quickly back to drag the dog ashore, then
dived into the waves once more and
swam off. The grateful words of the
bulldog followed him, "Goodbye,
Pinocchio! You saved my life!"

    The puppet swam on round the coast,
looking for a safe place to come ashore.

    At last, reaching a rocky headland,
Pinocchio saw a plume of smoke
rising from a dark cave. He
swam close to take a better
look, and was just about
to climb ashore when
suddenly he felt
himself being
hoisted clean
out of the
water. He had
been caught in a
fishing net and was
trapped in a shoal
of wriggling fish!
At that very
moment, a gigantic
fisherman emerged
from the cave.

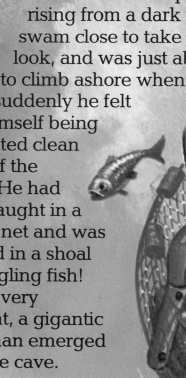
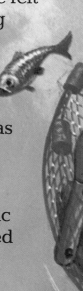
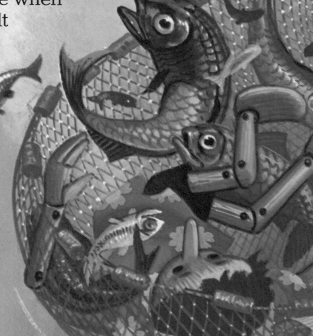

He was as ugly as a sea monster, and scaly all over. His head was covered with a thatch of seaweed, his scaly body was green, his bulging eyes were green and his beard was long and slimy.

"So, another good catch today," he growled, hauling in the net. And he stamped back into the cave, where a huge frying pan was sizzling over the log fire.

"Now then, what have we got here? This mullet looks good." And one by one he seized the fish, dabbed them in the flour, and tossed them into the pan. "Oh, these sardines look delicious! And what beautiful whiting! But what's this? This is a new one!"

And he plucked poor Pinocchio out of the net, all dripping wet and shaking with fear.

"I'm not a fish, I'm a puppet! Please let me go! I won't taste very nice!"

"Let you go? You must be joking!

Do you think I'd miss the chance of tasting such a rare fish? I've never caught a puppet before!" He rolled Pinocchio slowly in the flour — well seasoned with salt and pepper — and held him over the pan.

Just then there was a great growl and in rushed Alidoro, drawn to the cave by the wonderful smell of cooking.

"Get out!" shouted the fisherman, trying to kick the dog.

"Save me, Alidoro!" cried Pinocchio, struggling pathetically in the giant's hand.

The faithful hound leaped into the air, snatched the floury puppet from the giant's grasp and bolted out of the cave.

Alidoro carried Pinocchio back to the beach where their adventure had started. "There!" he said. "You save me first — now I've saved you. In this world we must all help each other." And Alidoro licked the puppet warmly before heading off again in search of his masters.

It was late in the day now, and Pinocchio was eager to get home. The road to the village took him past an old man's cottage, where he was told that the injured boy had recovered and that the police were no longer searching for him. It was a great relief, but the puppet was still worried about owning up to the Fairy.

"What on earth will she say?" he fretted. "I'm sure she will never forgive me. And it serves me right. I always promise to be good, but I never keep my word.

I'll never become a *real* boy!"

By the time Pinocchio reached the Fairy's house, night had fallen and he was cold and tired and very hungry. But when he knocked on the door, there was silence. Had the Fairy left him again? He waited and waited. At last, after half an hour, a window opened at the top of the house, and a big snail looked out, with a lighted lamp balanced on her head.

"Who's there at this time of night?" she asked.

"It's me, Pinocchio. Is the Fairy home?"

"The Fairy is asleep and must not be woken. But I will come down and let you in."

An hour passed, and then two, but still the door did not open. Pinocchio was freezing cold, so he knocked again. This time a window on the third floor opened. The snail looked out again. "My dear boy, there's no use knocking like that. I'm a snail — and snails never hurry." And she pulled the window shut.

Shortly afterwards, midnight struck, then one o'clock, and then two — and the door was still closed.

Poor Pinocchio! There was nothing he could do but wait. He stood there by the door all night, until at dawn the door finally opened. The snail had taken nine hours to come all the way downstairs!

"You cannot come in yet," she said. "The Fairy is still asleep."

"Then at least bring me something to

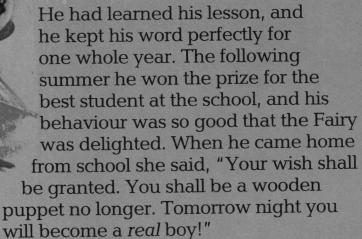

eat!" pleaded the puppet, "I'm starving!"

"At once," said the snail — and she returned two hours later with bread, roast chicken and fruit, all on a silver tray. Pinocchio tore hungrily at the food, but to his horror he found that none of it was real. It was all made of cardboard! Exhausted by all his dreadful ordeals, he fainted.

When he came to, he was lying on a sofa inside the house, with the Fairy beside him. She was not angry, but she gave Pinocchio a solemn warning: "You know you've done wrong. I will pardon you once more. But woe betide you if you behave badly a third time . . ."

Pinocchio promised again and again to change his ways for ever. And this time he meant it. He never wanted to go through a day and night like that again!

He had learned his lesson, and he kept his word perfectly for one whole year. The following summer he won the prize for the best student at the school, and his behaviour was so good that the Fairy was delighted. When he came home from school she said, "Your wish shall be granted. You shall be a wooden puppet no longer. Tomorrow night you will become a *real* boy!"

In bed that night, Pinocchio could hardly sleep he was so excited. Only one more day! If only he could be good for just one more day!

"But I've come to invite you to my party. Haven't you heard? At midnight I shall become a *real boy*!"

"Much good that will do you," sneered Candlewick. "Look, forget your silly party and come with me to Playland. It's the best place in the world. There are no schools and no teachers, and all you do is play from morning to night!"

"No, no, I can't. I'm late already, and I promised the Fairy I would be home before dark."

"Don't worry about her. All she ever does is scold you, anyway." And Candlewick told Pinocchio all about the fabulous land where summer holidays last all year.

But twilight was falling now, and Pinocchio turned to walk home. Then, suddenly, in the distance, there was the sound of a bugle. The coach was coming! Lights twinkled in the darkness, and there it was — pulled by four donkeys, all wearing white leather boots!

Dozens of boys were packed inside, all chatting excitedly. The jolly coachman — a little round man with a face like a tomato and a laughing mouth — hauled

"Just think, Pinocchio," said the Fairy. "At midnight you'll become a *real boy*! We must have a party to celebrate. Run out now and invite all your friends to come round. But don't be long. Make sure you're back before dark."

"I'll be back. I promise!" shouted the happy puppet, and he raced out of the house, jumping and dancing as he went.

Pinocchio ran from door to door, spreading his good news. Everyone promised to come to the party. But his very best friend — a lazy scamp they all called Candlewick because he was so thin — was nowhere to be found.

Pinocchio kept on searching. He ran right through all the streets three times — and eventually found his friend sitting just outside the village.

"What are you doing here?" asked Pinocchio.

"I'm waiting for the magic coach, which comes past here at nightfall. And then I'm going far, far away."

Candlewick on board, then turned to Pinocchio. "And what about you, my lad? Are you coming with us, or are you staying behind?

"I must go home, sir. I'm already late, and the Fairy will be cross with me."

No, no! Come with us to Playland!" called the boys from the coach. "Remember, no more school! No more teachers! Fun and games from morning to night!"

Pinocchio just could not resist. He gave a deep sigh, then said quietly, "All right, *I'll come!*"

The coach was so crowded that there was no room inside, so Pinocchio tried to climb on to a donkey. At once the animal reared up and kicked him into the road! All the boys giggled as Pinocchio angrily climbed up again from the other side. And again the donkey kicked

him off! The coachman was furious. He jumped down into the road and gave it a hearty whack with his stick. Then he lifted Pinocchio on to the animal's back. All through the long night's journey the poor donkey was in tears, and it kept whispering to Pinocchio, in a voice rather like a small boy's: "You stupid puppet! One day you'll be crying too. You never listen to good advice. You'll come to a bad end, like me. Just you wait and see!"

The coach rattled along hour after hour until, just after sunrise, it rolled into Playland. what a fabulous sight it was! There were boys playing everywhere you looked — running and jumping, shouting and laughing, playing with toys and balls and skates and bicycles. Some were dressed as soldiers, others made up like clowns. There were playgrounds and carousels, sandpits and theatres. The whole place was such a riot of fun that the new boys jumped straight down from the coach and plunged into the thick of it! How happy they all were!

The weeks passed like lightning. Pinocchio spent every minute playing, and never once regretted leaving home. "What a wonderful life!" said the puppet each time he met his friend. "And to think you wanted to go back to the Fairy," laughed Candlewick. "You're lucky to have me for a friend."

Then, one morning, after months of bliss, Pinocchio woke up to the most unpleasant shock he had ever had. His ears were long and brown and hairy — just like a donkey's!

The poor puppet was so ashamed that he burst into tears, and beat his head against the wall.

But the more he cried, the longer his ears grew! Finally, in despair, he pulled a long cotton cap right over his head to hide his ears and rushed off to find Candlewick.

At first his friend would not let him in and Pinocchio had to wait outside. But after half an hour the door slowly opened. And there stood Candlewick with a cap just like Pinocchio's, pulled right down over *his* long, hairy ears! You can imagine how foolish the two boys felt. For a few moments they stood in the middle of the room in silence. But then, instead of crying or consoling each other, they burst out laughing! At the count of three, they tore off their caps and threw them into the air and they started capering around the room, giggling and waggling their long hairy ears.

They laughed and laughed, until suddenly Candlewick stopped laughing and fell to his knees. Pinocchio looked down at him in amazement, then collapsed himself. Kneeling on the ground, they watched in horror as their hands turned into hooves, their faces lengthened into muzzles, and their backs sprouted coats of thick hair. And, worst of all, they each grew a long tail!

Then came a loud knock at the door. "Open up at once!

You donkeys belong to me!" And the coachman just kicked open the door and marched in.

He put bridles around their necks and led them off to the market place. Candlewick was bought by a farmer, who sent him to work in the fields. And Pinocchio was sold to a circus. The circus ringmaster was not a cruel man, but he would not stand for any nonsense. When his new donkey refused to eat hay, he struck him with a whip. And then he drove Pinocchio into the circus ring and taught him to jump through hoops, to dance waltzes and polkas, and to stand upright on his hind legs.

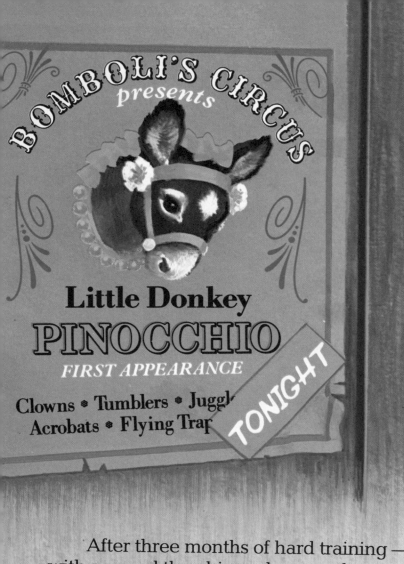

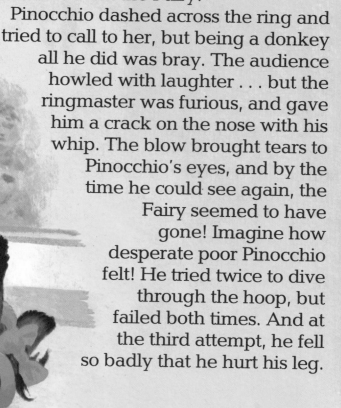

After three months of hard training — with a sound thrashing whenever he jumped badly — Pinocchio gave his first public performance. People came from miles around to see the amazing donkey, and the circus was packed an hour before the start.

The ringmaster cracked his whip, and in ran Pinocchio, the star attraction. He went round and round the ring, trotting, cantering, galloping. As the crowd cheered wildly at his wonderful performance, Pinocchio raised his head in pride and looked round the audience. And who should he see but the Fairy!

Pinocchio dashed across the ring and tried to call to her, but being a donkey all he did was bray. The audience howled with laughter . . . but the ringmaster was furious, and gave him a crack on the nose with his whip. The blow brought tears to Pinocchio's eyes, and by the time he could see again, the Fairy seemed to have gone! Imagine how desperate poor Pinocchio felt! He tried twice to dive through the hoop, but failed both times. And at the third attempt, he fell so badly that he hurt his leg.

It was a disaster for the circus. The very next day, the ringmaster sent him straight back to the market, where a drum-maker who wanted a donkey skin to make a drum bought poor, hungry Pinocchio for just ten pence. Then the man led the crippled donkey down to the sea-shore. Tying a rope to his muzzle, he pushed him into the water to drown!

He was free again, and safe. Now if only he could find the dear Fairy . . .

After half an hour the drum-maker hauled in the rope, thinking the donkey must be quite dead by now. But when he gave one final tug, instead of a dead donkey, he pulled out Pinocchio struggling and wriggling like an eel!

The poor man could not believe his eyes. He had thrown in a donkey — and pulled out a puppet.

"Where's my donkey?" he yelled.

"I'm your donkey!" laughed Pinocchio. "The fishes nibbled away at the carcass — and left only me! They must have been summoned by the Fairy!"

And with a cheeky wave, he slipped the rope from his nose and dived into the sea.

Pinocchio was in such a hurry to escape from Playland and the drum-maker that he swam far out to sea, until all that could be seen of him was a tiny black speck on the horizon. He was so happy to be free that every now and then he swung his legs out of the water and waggled them above the surface, like a dolphin's tail.

He swam for hours, not really caring which way he went. Then, suddenly, he glimpsed a strange sight. Towering out of the waves was a rock of pure white marble, and on the top stood a beautiful little goat, which was bleating to him in a very friendly way, and nodding excitedly.

Most surprising of all, the goat's hair was blue! And Pinocchio realised that it was not a normal goat at all, but his Good Fairy in disguise, come to rescue him again.

His heart began beating at twice its usual rate, and he swam towards the goat with all his strength. But before he was halfway to the marble rock, a huge monster

42

shark reared up and out of the water! Pinocchio felt himself drawn helplessly towards its massive mouth, and its three rows of enormous jagged teeth!

Just think of Pinocchio's terror! He struggled to change direction. He cried piteously for help. And the blue goat called out in anguish, "Swim quickly Pinocchio! The shark will get you!"

But it was already too late! Gigantic jaws closed around the wriggling puppet, and everything went dark. Pinocchio felt himself sliding down the monster's throat, and into its vast stomach — and then he blacked out.

When Pinocchio came to, he was terribly scared. It was very dark, and eerily silent. From time to time there was a strange rasping noise, and great gusts of wind blew into his face. It was the shark breathing! Poor Pinocchio felt so lost and alone that he cried and screamed. "Help, help! Save me! Won't someone save me?"

Then, out of the gloom, came a low voice. "No-one will save you, unhappy wretch. You can do nothing but wait to be digested!"

"Who's that?" stammered Pinocchio, shaking with fear.

"It is I, a poor Tuna fish, who was swallowed by the shark just before you. But I do not cry or yell. I am a philosopher. I count myself lucky to be eaten by a fish, and not by humans!"

"But I don't want to be eaten at *all!*"

cried the puppet. "I want to escape! How big is this shark, and where's the way out?"

"There is no way out," replied the Tuna, with a voice of doom. "The shark is a mile long — and that's not counting his tail!"

Left alone with the Tuna, Pinocchio might have given up hope, but while they were talking he saw a tiny light twinkling in the distance. So, saying goodbye, he groped his way along the body of the shark. It took a long time for him to reach the flickering light, but when he finally arrived, he could hardly believe his eyes.

He found a little old man, with a long white beard, sitting at a table with a lighted candle stuck into a bottle!

And who do you think the old man was? Yes, it was Geppetto, the wood-carver — Pinocchio's own dear father! The puppet was overcome with joy.

"Oh Daddy, Daddy, I've found you at last, after all this time."

And he did not know whether to laugh or cry at the old man's astonished face.

"Do my old eyes deceive me? Is it really you, Pinocchio? I thought I had lost you forever." And he hugged his son as if he would never let go. "I have been in this shark for two years, since that fateful day when I set sail in my little boat. I saw the white dove leave you on the beach, and

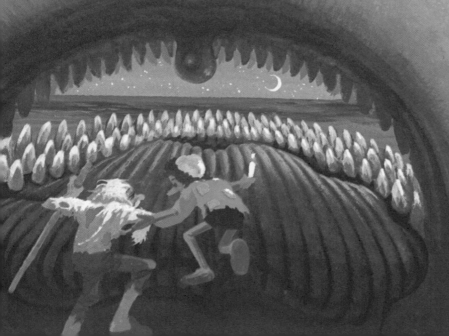

tried hard to return to shore. But the waves blew up and hurled me to the shark!"

"But how have you survived, Daddy?"

"In that same dreadful storm, a merchant ship was wrecked and the shark swallowed all its cargo. For these two years I have lived off the ship's supplies — corned beef, biscuits, cheese and sugar. There were even bottles of wine. But now I have nothing left and this is the very last candle!"

Hearing this, Pinocchio was more determined than ever to escape. Taking the candle in one hand, he led his poor father off into the darkness. For more than an hour they struggled along the belly of the shark, until they arrived at the back of the monster's mouth.

Peering through, beyond the jagged teeth, they could see the bright moon and a starry sky.

The shark was fast asleep, with his mouth wide open.

"Quick, Daddy, we must get out before the monster wakes!"

And, as the shark's snoring thundered in their ears, they climbed silently along its tongue, across its rows of teeth, and out on to its giant lip.

Then Pinocchio took Geppetto on his shoulders, leaped into the water, and swam away. The sea was calm and silent . . . and the shark was still sleeping like a log!

Pinocchio swam for hours, carrying his poor father — who could not swim a stroke. When dawn broke, the puppet was getting very tired and there was still no sign of land. Then, just as he felt he could move his arms and legs no more, he heard a familiar voice. "No need to panic. I will have you on dry land in a few minutes."

It was the Tuna. And as Pinocchio and Geppetto clambered thankfully on to his back, he explained how he had followed their example and escaped from the snoring shark.

The awful dangers were finally over. The Tuna left them safely on a sandy beach

and Pinocchio thanked him again and again. Then the puppet and his father walked slowly inland, looking for food and shelter.

They had not gone far when they met two creatures begging by the roadside. They were the Fox and the Cat, who had fallen on hard times.

The Fox really *had* gone lame, and the Cat really *had* gone blind.

"Dear Pinocchio," whined the Fox. "Give a little charity to the needy!"

"Yes, my dear boy," pleaded the Cat. "Do help the aged and infirm!"

But Pinocchio and Geppetto ignored the wicked pair. "If you are poor now, you deserve it. You won't catch me out again!"

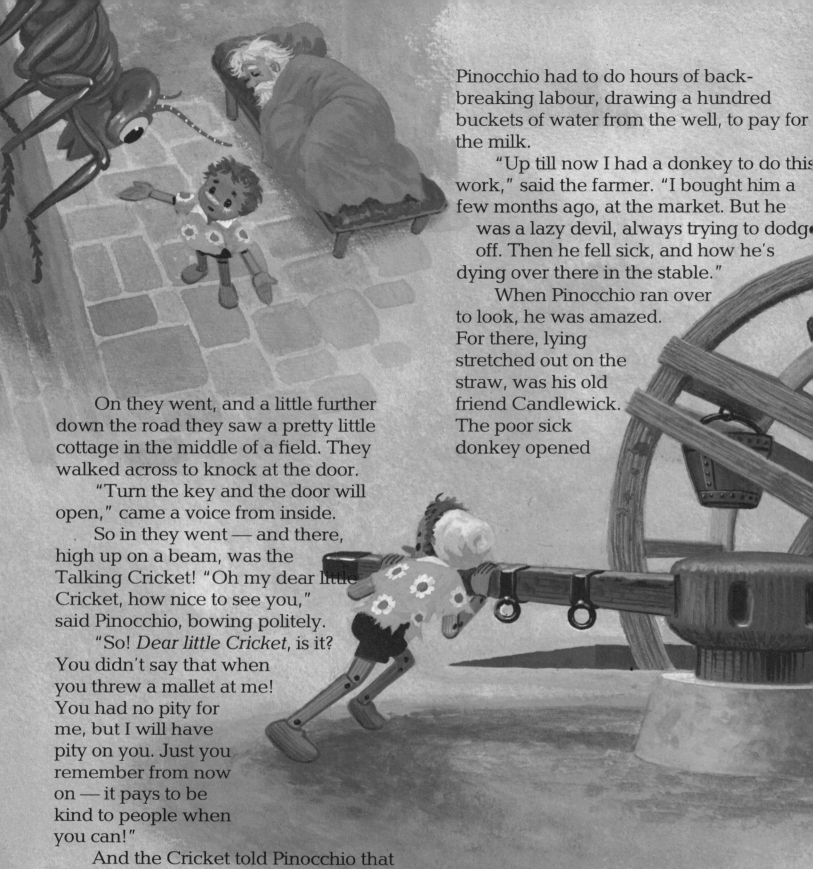

Pinocchio had to do hours of back-breaking labour, drawing a hundred buckets of water from the well, to pay for the milk.

"Up till now I had a donkey to do this work," said the farmer. "I bought him a few months ago, at the market. But he was a lazy devil, always trying to dodge off. Then he fell sick, and how he's dying over there in the stable."

When Pinocchio ran over to look, he was amazed. For there, lying stretched out on the straw, was his old friend Candlewick. The poor sick donkey opened

On they went, and a little further down the road they saw a pretty little cottage in the middle of a field. They walked across to knock at the door.

"Turn the key and the door will open," came a voice from inside.

So in they went — and there, high up on a beam, was the Talking Cricket! "Oh my dear little Cricket, how nice to see you," said Pinocchio, bowing politely.

"So! *Dear little Cricket*, is it? You didn't say that when you threw a mallet at me! You had no pity for me, but I will have pity on you. Just you remember from now on — it pays to be kind to people when you can!"

And the Cricket told Pinocchio that he had been given the cottage the day before by a beautiful blue-haired goat, who had gone away bleating in sorrow about a puppet that had been swallowed by a shark.

Deeply moved, and determined to be good, the puppet helped his tired father to lie down on a bed of straw, then went off in search of milk for him to drink. A nearby farmer offered him a jug, but only at a price.

his eyes for the last time, gave a deep, groaning sigh . . . and died.

From then on, for many months Pinocchio worked for the farmer every day from dawn to dusk, to buy milk for his father and earn a few extra pennies for their daily needs. He learned to weave baskets from reeds and,

46

whenever he could, he practised reading and writing. He worked so hard that after six months he had managed to save up fifty pence. So the next morning he set off for the market to buy himself a new shirt.

It was a beautiful day. The sun was shining and the birds were singing in the trees. The puppet was scampering along merrily, when all at once he saw a big snail, who called out to him, "Pinocchio! Stop!"

It was the Fairy's Snail, who had taken so long to let the puppet into her house the evening after he had been caught by the giant green fisherman!

"My beautiful Snail! What are you doing here? Do you know where the Fairy is?"

"Oh Pinocchio, the poor Fairy is very ill in hospital, and is likely to die! She has no money left to buy herself food."

At once the puppet snatched the fifty pence from his pocket and gave the coins to the Snail. "Quickly, take this money to the Fairy! I don't need a new shirt — these rags are enough for me." Without another word, the Snail raced off at high speed — quite unlike her normal self.

Pinocchio went straight back to the cottage and started work. Now he had *two* people to support — Geppetto *and* the Fairy. He slaved away making baskets

until midnight, then curled up on his bed of straw and fell sound asleep.

And, as he slept, he dreamed he saw the Fairy. She was more beautiful than ever. She smiled at him, and kissed him gently. Then she said softly, "You're a good boy, Pinocchio. You have worked hard for Geppetto and for me in our time of need. I forgive you all your naughty past. And I promise you that if you are good in the future, you will always be happy."

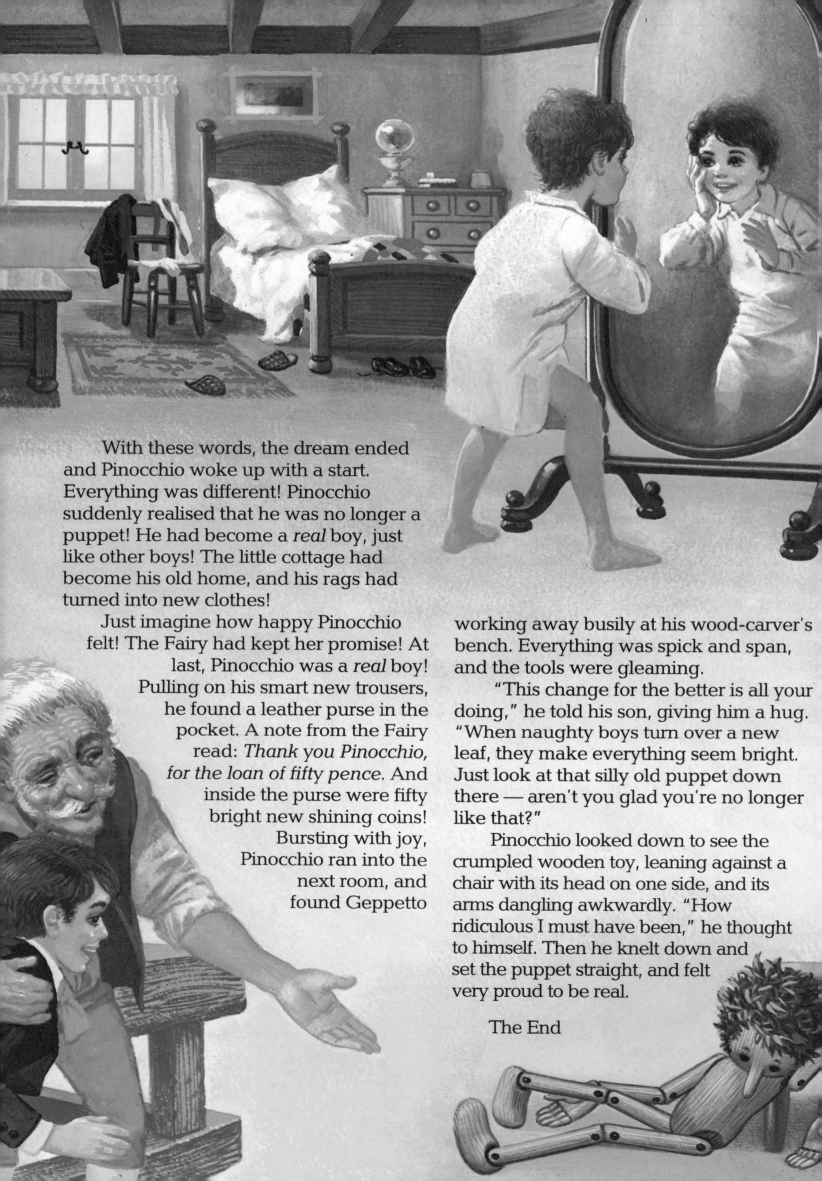

With these words, the dream ended and Pinocchio woke up with a start. Everything was different! Pinocchio suddenly realised that he was no longer a puppet! He had become a *real* boy, just like other boys! The little cottage had become his old home, and his rags had turned into new clothes!

Just imagine how happy Pinocchio felt! The Fairy had kept her promise! At last, Pinocchio was a *real* boy! Pulling on his smart new trousers, he found a leather purse in the pocket. A note from the Fairy read: *Thank you Pinocchio, for the loan of fifty pence.* And inside the purse were fifty bright new shining coins!

Bursting with joy, Pinocchio ran into the next room, and found Geppetto working away busily at his wood-carver's bench. Everything was spick and span, and the tools were gleaming.

"This change for the better is all your doing," he told his son, giving him a hug. "When naughty boys turn over a new leaf, they make everything seem bright. Just look at that silly old puppet down there — aren't you glad you're no longer like that?"

Pinocchio looked down to see the crumpled wooden toy, leaning against a chair with its head on one side, and its arms dangling awkwardly. "How ridiculous I must have been," he thought to himself. Then he knelt down and set the puppet straight, and felt very proud to be real.

The End

Box of Robbers

Martha was all alone in the house and feeling very bored. "I know," she thought after a while, "I'll fetch my doll's house from the attic and play with that." So she climbed the stairs to the little room under the roof. Inside there were boxes and trunks, piles of old carpet, furniture and bundles of clothing. And in a dusty corner she found her doll's house.

Martha was about to pick it up, when she noticed the black wooden chest her Uncle Walter had sent from Italy. Martha had been told there was no key, and that Uncle Walter had forbidden anyone to open it.

It was a big chest, studded with big brass nails. Martha longed to see what was in it. "Oh, if only I had a key . . ." she thought. Then, she remembered the big basket of keys on the shelf in the linen cupboard. Perhaps one of them would unlock the mysterious chest?

Martha tried one key after another. At last, an ancient brass key slipped into the lock. Martha heard a click — and as the lid flew up, she jumped back in amazement.

49

Slowly and carefully, a man stepped out, stretched himself, then bowed to her politely. He was tall and thin and his face was suntanned.

Then, another man emerged from the chest, yawning. He was middle-sized, and his skin was as tanned as the first.

While Martha stared, open-mouthed, a third man crawled out of the chest. He had a suntan, too, but was short and fat.

And they all wore long, red velvet jackets, braided with gold, and sky-blue satin breeches. Their hats had broad brims and ribbons fluttered from the crowns. They had big, gold rings in their

ears and knives and pistols in their belts. Their black eyes glittered, and they wore long, curling moustaches.

"My! You were heavy!" exclaimed the fat one. "You squeezed me out of shape."

"There's no need to be disagreeable," said the middle-sized man.

"Permit us to introduce ourselves," said the thin man to Martha. "This is Luigi," — the fat man nodded. "And this is Beni," — the middle-sized man bowed. "And I am Victor. We're Italian bandits."

"Bandits!" cried Martha, in horror.

"Perhaps in all the world there are

not three bandits more terrible and fierce," boasted Beni.

"That's true," said Luigi nodding.

"But . . . it's wicked!" cried Martha.

"You're right," said Victor. "We're extremely wicked."

"That's true," said Luigi nodding. "But it's . . . it's naughty!" said Martha.

"Naughty?" gasped Beni with a horrified look. "I little thought to be called that — and by a lady! Oh! Oh! But how are we to be bandits, unless we're wicked?"

"Well, stop being bandits!"

Luigi sat down on an old chair and wiped his forehead with a yellow silk scarf. Beni and Victor stared at Martha with pale faces.

"But what shall we do for a living?" all three said.

"Oh there's lots to do. You could drive a bus or be a clerk — or, or become policemen."

"Policemen?" they said, shaking their heads. "But our business is to rob."

Martha tried to think. "I know it's hard, but you could try."

"No!" cried Beni. "Bandits we have always been and bandits we must remain! There are always people to rob!"

"Brothers!" said Victor, suddenly. "Let's rob the house we're in!"

"Of course!" shouted the others. Beni turned to Martha. "Stay here! If you stir one step, your blood will flow. But don't worry — I don't really mean it. That's just the way bandits talk. Of course we would never ever hurt such a nice young lady as you."

Then the three crept quietly down the stairs with cocked pistols, and knives between their teeth.

When they came back, Luigi was carrying a pile of Martha's best dresses. Victor had a brass candlestick and the kitchen clock. And Beni carried a box of knives and forks and an old coat.

"How wonderful it is to rob once more!" said Victor. And all three sat on the floor and munched the cake and sipped the wine they had stolen from the pantry.

Then, the doorbell rang. Beni, Victor and Luigi scrambled to their feet, daggers drawn.

Martha ran to the window, and saw that it was only the postman, delivering a letter. But it gave her an idea.

"Oh! Oh, it's the police!" she cried.

The robbers looked at each other and trembled. "Are there many of them?"

I don't understand. Perhaps its those cakes we ate."

"Could be," answered Luigi's voice.

So Martha sat on the lid and pressed it down with all her weight. With a click the chest snapped shut. And with a broad, happy smile, Martha turned the old brass key.

Now this story should teach us not to interfere with things that do not concern us. Because if Martha had not opened Uncle Walter's chest, she would not have had to carry all the robber's plunder downstairs.

"A hundred and twelve!" exclaimed Martha after pretending to count.

"Then we are lost!" declared Beni.

"Are they armed?"

"Oh yes," said Martha, "with guns and swords and pistols and axes and . . . and . . . cannons!"

All three groaned, but Beni said, "I hope they kill us quickly."

"You are my friends, aren't you?" said Martha turning from the window. "Then I shall save you. I suggest you get back into the chest. I'll close the lid, then the police won't find you. But you must be quick! They'll soon be here!"

Into the chest jumped Luigi, lying flat on the bottom. Next in went Beni and, pausing only to kiss Martha's hand, Victor lay on top. When they were all settled in, Martha pressed the lid down tightly. "Try pushing down more," she said. "Squeeze down more. Squeeze down."

"I'm doing my best," snapped Victor. "We fitted nicely before.

The Flying Piggy-Bank

My Mum gave me a smashing piggy-bank for my birthday. It was pink and round, with the word TAIWAN stamped on its underside in capital letters. I put it on the window-sill in my bedroom, and every week I put some of my pocket money through the slot on its back.

Then one day I decided I wanted to buy a new bed for my doll's house. I took down the piggy-bank, prised open the rubber plug underneath it and shook it hard over my bed.

Nothing came out. Not a penny.

"It's gone!" I shouted. "I've been putting money in here for weeks and it's all gone! Where's my money?"

"I ate it."

"What did you say?" I could hardly believe where the voice was coming from.

"You fed it to me, so I ate it," repeated the piggy-bank.

"Oh, you can talk, can you?"

"Yes, if someone talks to me."

"In that case you can tell me where my money is."

"I've told you, I ate it."

"But it's not in your stomach any more!"

"I've digested it," said Taiwan. "Where else do you think pigs like me get our energy from?"

"It's not good enough," I said, giving him another shake. "I want my poocket money! Give it back at once!"

"I can't" he said crossly. "We'll just have to go and get some more."

"Where from?" I asked.

"Well, where does money come from?" Taiwan said impatiently. "The Royal Mint, of course. The Royal Mint inside the Royal Palace of the Prince of Riches. If you climb on my back I'll fly you there. But you'll have to feed me first. I'm starving! And I can't fly on an empty stomach."

I fetched my collection of foreign coins and posted them into the slot.

With all this money the pig began to grow. He grew to such a size that he rolled off the window-sill, and soon a

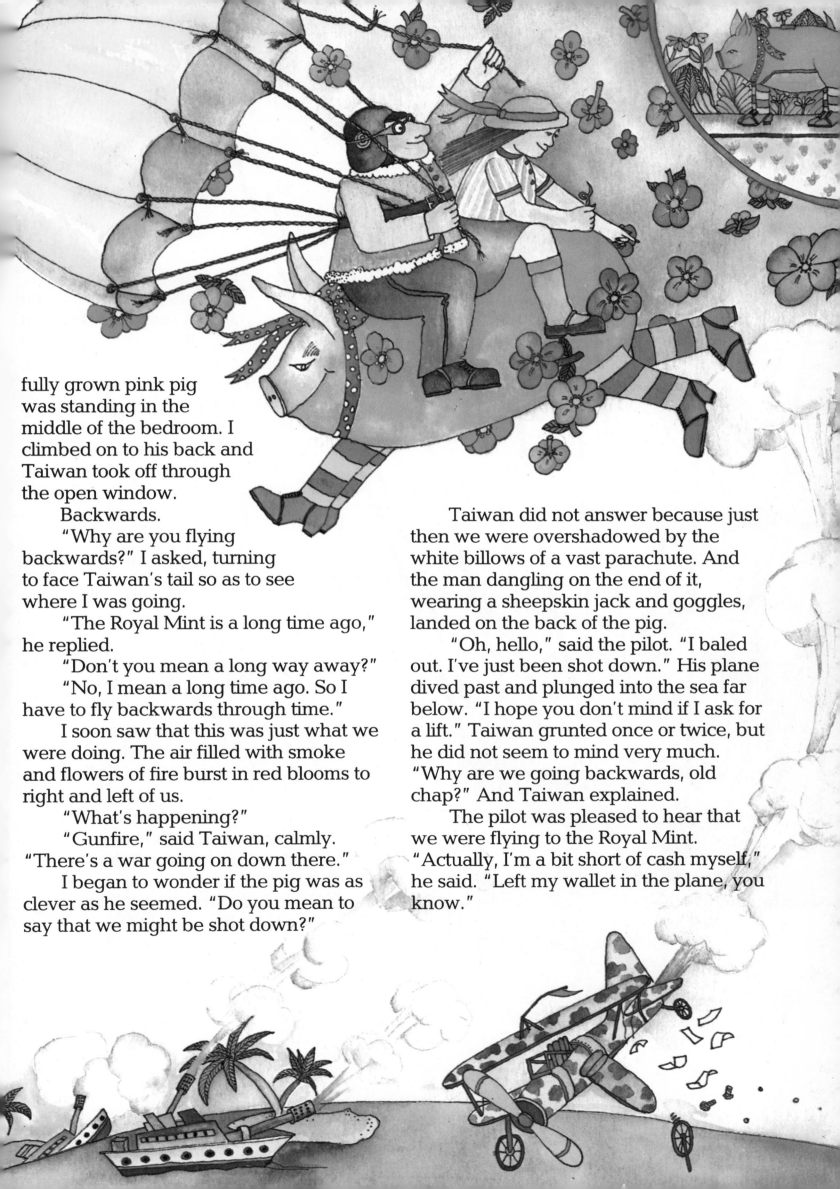

fully grown pink pig was standing in the middle of the bedroom. I climbed on to his back and Taiwan took off through the open window.

Backwards.

"Why are you flying backwards?" I asked, turning to face Taiwan's tail so as to see where I was going.

"The Royal Mint is a long time ago," he replied.

"Don't you mean a long way away?"

"No, I mean a long time ago. So I have to fly backwards through time."

I soon saw that this was just what we were doing. The air filled with smoke and flowers of fire burst in red blooms to right and left of us.

"What's happening?"

"Gunfire," said Taiwan, calmly. "There's a war going on down there."

I began to wonder if the pig was as clever as he seemed. "Do you mean to say that we might be shot down?"

Taiwan did not answer because just then we were overshadowed by the white billows of a vast parachute. And the man dangling on the end of it, wearing a sheepskin jack and goggles, landed on the back of the pig.

"Oh, hello," said the pilot. "I baled out. I've just been shot down." His plane dived past and plunged into the sea far below. "I hope you don't mind if I ask for a lift." Taiwan grunted once or twice, but he did not seem to mind very much. "Why are we going backwards, old chap?" And Taiwan explained.

The pilot was pleased to hear that we were flying to the Royal Mint. "Actually, I'm a bit short of cash myself," he said. "Left my wallet in the plane, you know."

Next we passed an explorer riding in the basket of a huge hot-air balloon. "It must be a hundred years earlier than yesterday," I thought, looking at his strange clothes and deerstalker hat. "Would you take me along with you?" he asked as we floated past. "The wind's blowing in the wrong direction and I shall never get where I'm going."

"If you come with us," I told him, "you only get to the Royal Mint." He seemed to like the idea and climbed aboard the pig in front of the pilot and behind me.

We must have flown another thousand years into the past when Taiwan suddenly tripped in mid-air. We all nearly fell off.

"What a silly place to leave string," he said grumpily. And with his feet tangled up in twine, he kept flying.

"Please to let go of kite," said a little voice far below us. We peered down and there, high above the ground, was a Chinaman hanging from the end of the string. Above us, his kite flapped

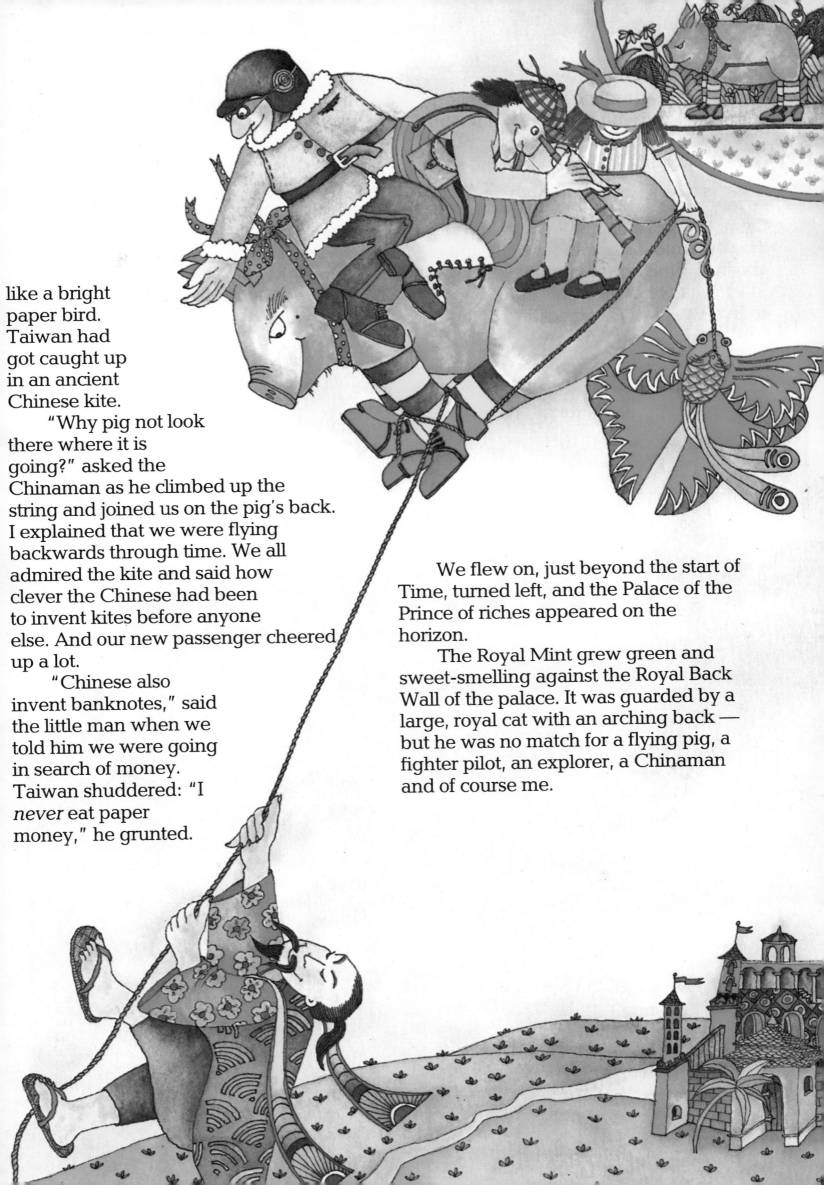

like a bright
paper bird.
Taiwan had
got caught up
in an ancient
Chinese kite.
    "Why pig not look
there where it is
going?" asked the
Chinaman as he climbed up the
string and joined us on the pig's back.
I explained that we were flying
backwards through time. We all
admired the kite and said how
clever the Chinese had been
to invent kites before anyone
else. And our new passenger cheered
up a lot.
    "Chinese also
invent banknotes," said
the little man when we
told him we were going
in search of money.
Taiwan shuddered: "I
never eat paper
money," he grunted.

    We flew on, just beyond the start of
Time, turned left, and the Palace of the
Prince of riches appeared on the
horizon.
    The Royal Mint grew green and
sweet-smelling against the Royal Back
Wall of the palace. It was guarded by a
large, royal cat with an arching back —
but he was no match for a flying pig, a
fighter pilot, an explorer, a Chinaman
and of course me.

While they were struggling and scrambling through the Royal Sage and Thyme. I crept in among the Royal Mint and picked the silver and copper coins that hung down from every plant, and stuffed my pockets with them. When Taiwan trotted up I posted the coins into his slot and we all climbed aboard for the return journey.

We flew forwards this time, of course, the pig's ears crackling in the wind. But with four passengers aboard, Taiwan was soon tired and hungry again.

"More money! More money!" he grunted, and I posted a handful of coins into his slot.

"I'm sorry," he said shortly. "But some of you must get off. You're just too heavy for me."

"That's quite all right, said the explorer. "My hot-air balloon has just come into sight. Look, it's over there."

The pilot decided to join the explorer

in his travels round the world. And the Chinaman drifted back to earth on the end of his kite string. So I was left all alone, riding the flying pig. But before we reached home, I had to feed every coin I had picked at the Royal Mint into Taiwan's slot.

"I'm still hungry!" he complained, and his empty stomach rumbled between my knees. I shut my eyes and wedged my fingers into his slot in case we crashed.

The next thing I knew, we had tumbled in through my bedroom window and the pig was lying on its side on the floor, small and stiff and shrunken back to its normal size.

I picked it up and shook it. Not a rattle. I peered down its slot. Not a penny. I ran into the kitchen and shouted to my mother. "There's no money left in the piggy-bank!"

"Yes dear, I'm sorry about that," she said. "I had to borrow it to pay the milkman. "Let's see —

how much was in there? Here you are."

She gave me two crisp green notes. I crinkled them in my hand, remembering that Taiwan did not eat paper money.

"Do you think that if I saved my pocket money every week . . ."

"Pigs might fly," said mother,
"Oh well," I said, "I will then!"

PETRUSHKA

The bells were ringing out all over Moscow. A mighty pealing chorus echoed far across the city. It was shrove Tuesday, the day of the great carnival.

Admiralty Square was packed with people, and there were entertainers everywhere — strongmen lifting massive bar-bells, bareback riders on nimble little ponies, sword-swallowers and fire-eaters, jugglers and dancers.

Most popular of all was a brightly coloured tent where a Showman was introducing his puppet show.

"The show you are about to witness, ladies and gentlemen, is a spectacle unmatched in all the Russias!" declared the Showman, his black eyes glinting beneath his fur hat. "The puppets you will see today are quite unlike any you have ever seen! They will come alive before your very eyes!"

With a flourish, the Showman flicked aside the curtain to reveal three magnificent puppets: the Moor, a dashing Moroccan prince; the Princess, a delicate ballerina; and Petrushka, a wicked-looking sailor.

"They're not alive!" came a hoarse shout from the back of the crowd, where a fat merchant was winking at two gypsy girls. "Tell us another one. Hah!"

But with a withering glance, the Showman pulled from his deep pocket a tiny silver flute and touched each puppet in turn

upon the shoulder. Instantly, they sprang to their feet, and as the Showman played a lively tune they danced and twisted about on the little stage.

At the end of the dance, the crowd cheered with delight — and with a loud guffaw, the merchant threw a pile of rouble notes high into the air! The gypsy girls jumped to catch them, but the Showman silenced everyone with a long, low note from the flute.

The puppets stood as if bewitched. Then the showman began playing a slow, mysterious tune and the Moor stood proudly at one side of the stage, his hands on his hips. The Princess stood in the centre, smiling radiantly, and Petrushka fell to his knees, as if pleading with her.

"The ugly sailor Petrushka loves the Princess," said the Showman. "But she rejects him."

The ballerina turned to the Moor and took his arm. They strolled together at the edge of the stage, looking deep into each other's eyes. Then, Petrushka, snarling like a tiger, pulled out a cudgel and ran across the stage. He tried to attack his rival, but the Moor bravely stepped in front of the Princess and knocked the cudgel from the sailor's hand.

Petrushka crawled back across the stage, then turned and begged for mercy. But the ballerina took the Moor's arm and walked with him to the centre of the stage. Ignoring poor Petrushka, they hugged each other and bowed deeply to the crowd.

"Thus the Moor marries the Princess and the sailor becomes their servant," boomed the showman, and he swept the curtain back across the stage. "The last show will be at four o'clock." Then he walked through the crowd, collecting coins in his fur hat.

dressing rooms, the puppets were stirring.

Petrushka the ugly sailor was in tears. "How I hate that Showman," he cried. "why did he make me so ugly, and the Princess so beautiful? If only I was handsome, like the Moor, or I could dance like him! Then perhaps she might love me instead!" Then perhaps she might love me instead!" He jerked to his feet and took a few, awkward steps towards the stage. "I must learn to dance, I must! Then I will kill the Moor, and marry the Princess.

At that moment Petrushka noticed the ballerina watching him from her room. She danced towards him on the tips of her toes, as graceful and as delicate as a bird. Petrushka's heart pounded, and he tried desperately to dance beside her, but it was no good. He tripped over his feet and fell to the floor.

The ballerina soon got bored with watching his clumsy efforts. So she danced away again, along the stage.

The Moor in his dressing room was practising with his scimitar in front of a mirror. He strode manfully up and down, and cut and slashed and lunged. But when the ballerina danced in, the Moor sprang to attention. He clapped merrily

The Showman sat down on a bench behind the theatre, and counted his money. It had been a good day, all right! Five shows already, and plenty of coins in the hat! He gave a deep, throaty chuckle, and closed his eyes for a nap.

But behind the curtain, in their

and stamped his feet
as she glided
towards him.
Then they spun
around together
in a wild, Eastern
dance.

Suddenly
Petrushka burst in. He had
been watching them from
the stage and he could not bear to see his
beloved ballerina dancing with the Moor.
"Take your hands off my Princess!" he
shouted. And he charged at the Moor,
brandishing his cudgel.

Outside the theatre, a crowd was
gathering for the last show of the day.
The golden domes threw long shadows
across the square, but many people had
stayed late to see the famous puppet
show. The merchant was back again,
with his two gypsy girls, and there was

even a performing bear
with his trainer! They all
gathered in a semi-circle
and waited patiently while
the Showman recited his speech:
"Ladies and gentlemen, the
puppets you will see today are
unlike any you have ever seen.
They will come alive before your . . ."

But, at that moment, the curtains
burst open behind the Showman's back.
Petrushka leaped down from the stage
and ran away full pelt across the square.
Behind him rushed the Moor, in a furious
rage, waving the scimitar above his head.
As the crowd turned in astonishment,
Petrushka slipped and fell. Down came
the scimitar in a great, flashing arc, and
Petrushka lay deadly still, face down in
the snow.

"They're alive!" shouted the merchant. There's been a murder!"

But the Showman snatched up the Moor and Petrushka, and shook and slapped them. A trail of sawdust trickled down from Petrushka's face. "There you are," he whined. "Just puppets. But there'll be no more shows today, ladies and gentleman."

As the crowd drifted away, the Showman thrust the two puppets in through the back of the theatre and closed the tent. Then he walked off to a tavern, shaking his head gloomily.

Later that night he returned to the theatre. He drew back the curtain, and peered inside. There was the ballerina, sleeping in her room.

The Moor sat cross-legged on the stage, quitely polishing his scimitar. On the floor lay Petrushka, broken and torn.

"What was that?" gasped the Showman. Something was moving in the darkness above the theatre. He looked up and saw in the moonlight — the ghost of Petrushka, dancing in the air. It shook its fist and scowled at the Showman.

"You made me ugly!" it snarled. "You made a fool of me! But now it's my turn, I'm free of the body you made for me. Now I can dance as well as anyone. Watch me! My love for the ballerina has made my spirit delicate and free. But my ugliness will haunt you for the rest of your days! And his laughter echoed in the frosty air.